Maybe If I Loved You More

OTHER BOOKS BY JAMES KAVANAUGH

Maybe If I Loved You More

James Kavanaugh

E. P. DUTTON · NEW YORK

*Published in the United States by
E. P. Dutton, Inc.,
2 Park Avenue,
New York, N.Y. 10016*

Library of Congress Cataloging in Publication Data
Kavanaugh, James J.
Maybe if I loved you more.
   I. Title.
PS3561.A88M3   1982   *811'.54*   *82-5095*
ISBN: 0-525-24133-7   *AACR2*

*Published simultaneously in Canada by
Clarke, Irwin & Company Limited, Toronto and Vancouver*

Designed by Nicola Mazzella

10   9   8   7   6   5   4   3

*To my brother, Bob, who died
this year and left an
irreplaceable void.*

To Rene

*To those who finally understand
that without love, life
means nothing.*

Introduction

So much of life is spent trying to prove something. It begins in childhood and never seems to end. Trying to prove we're bigger or stronger, better or richer or smarter. Trying to prove that we deserve someone's love. But feeling secretly that we don't.

MAYBE IF I LOVED YOU MORE, I wouldn't have to prove anything.

So much of life is spent in fear. From the simple dares of childhood to the complex ones of the adult. Fear of failure, fear of losing a job or ending a relationship, fear of marriage or divorce, fear of sickness or aging, fear of love or death.

MAYBE IF I LOVED YOU MORE, I wouldn't have to be afraid.

So much of life is spent in isolation. From the lonely daydreams of a child to the unuttered secrets of an adult. Isolated in our dreams, in our thoughts, in the midst of a crowd, isolated especially in our anxieties and hurts and private rages.

MAYBE IF I LOVED YOU MORE, I wouldn't have to feel alone.

So much of life is spent in guilt. From the first sadness in a parent's eye to the tears of a lover. Guilt over working too hard or not hard enough, guilt over loving too much or not enough. Guilt over children that love us and those that don't. Guilt over money or God or our most satisfying dreams.

MAYBE IF I LOVED YOU MORE, I wouldn't have to feel guilty.

So much of life is spent in an effort to be loved. We beg for it from infancy. We struggle to please everyone, parents, teachers, neighbors, anyone who seems important. We do it all our lives. Success becomes the measure of our worth. Even the simplest failure can mean that we are not really lovable.

MAYBE IF I LOVED YOU MORE,
                Finally I would be loved!

James Kavanaugh
Los Gatos, California

10

Maybe If I Loved You More

Why Is It?

Why is it
   I barely remember that you sent me to college
     and bought my clothes,
   Slaved like a peddler to live in a neighborhood
     with all the best WASPs
   Taught me that an education would admit me
     to every king's court in the world
   Far quicker than power or money?
Well, you were wrong about all that,
   But then you didn't make up the rules
     and I haven't met five like you
   Since you died.
But why is it
   I remember so clearly the Mounted Policeman's suit
     you gave me when I was six,
   And the doctor set I didn't expect when I was seven?
Why is it
   That these and your smile
   Make me love you more than all the rest?

Arthur

Arthur found Jesus—or so he told me—
    Not in clouds or a green forest grown gold in the setting sun,
    Not even in a swamp grown silver in an alchemist's moonlight,
       But in some prolonged, secret embrace
       Where Jesus was all his and he was all Jesus'.
I recognize that these are hard times
    And a man has to find his solace where he can,
But I'd feel better about Arthur
    If after his conversion he'd pick up a lunch check once in a while.
And I'd feel much better about Jesus
    If He'd save just one person I admire.

Like the Boy

Will nothing make me feel like the boy who drank cold Pepsis on a
  summer afternoon,
Who fell into bed at night with delicious exhaustion, moaning with
  pleasure beyond sex or success?
I am tired of tax shelters, bored with write-offs, weary of properties I do
  not want, sick of financial revenge and a strong portfolio.
How does an honest man live upon the earth? What does he eat, or
  does it matter? Where does he live, or does it matter?
To whom does he give away his luxury, or is it only important that he
  be rid of it?
I stand soft among a soft people, hear the bleatings about inflation and
  the sinking dollar,
Wanting some discipline my life does not provide, some community
  beyond man and beast.
Happiness for me is not a state of rest, but of motion. Not some qui-
  etude, but an energy. Not a peace, but a passion
I want to believe in far more than a God who settles things at the end,
Or a country that is as unprincipled and vacillating as I am.
There is no rite of passage anymore, nothing that makes a boy a man,
Certainly nothing that makes a man a man and keeps him there.
How do I want to live the rest of my life upon the earth?
What inspires me and brings me peace? Another book? Another build-
  ing? Another business? Enough of that!
I want to start a war! A war that will kill no one save the passionless
  part of me that drifts and flounders on the earth,
So that I might once again feel like the boy who drank cold Pepsis on a
  summer afternoon and fell into bed with delicious exhaustion.

It Is No Triumph

It is no triumph to be admired
  Like a mountain peak or pine forest,
  Like waves whipped frothy by the wind,
  Or a swampland frozen motionless at midnight.
Admiration knows nothing of dawn's tears
  And the gathered fears of a confused lifetime.
Nor is it any solace
  When a brother is dying and life is trying
    To make a mockery of all I've become.
Cowards and braggards are as admired as brave men,
Liars and charlatans are as esteemed as the truly honorable,
  Because admiration sees but the surface
  And is lulled by the spell of one's own imaginings.
Tonight it is enough to be admired by no one,
To rest in your arms and to know that you love me enough
  To read the dim corners of my eyes,
  To hear the pauses on my lips,
  To rest together in a silence
Where there is nothing to admire
  And everything to love.

The Caterpillar

What other men
  Somehow knew
I have had to learn
  Like a curious caterpillar
    Crawling over every branch,
    Inspecting every leaf,
  Lost in a world of my own making
And crying my caterpillar tears
  Softly.

I Have Feared Love

I have feared love
  With all its hidden demands
  With its misty promises and drying skin
  With its moist eyes and my own deepest concern
      That once I settled on one,
  I might finally find the other destined for me.
I feared love because I may have waited too long
  And kept intact the memory of too much pain at its passing.
Finally I have lived long enough to know that such fear
  Is groundless, pale, passionless compared to the fear
    Of never having known love at all.
That is fear, indeed, to wake up each morning without anyone
  To share the day or a cup of coffee (or is it Sanka now, love?)
To settle into the darkest night without cuddling or caring
  Or knowing that to one I am worth life itself. And more.
I watched my father die and wondered what he shared with my mother,
Wondered how two so often silent and distant could endure fifty years.
Now I know, because my own life has crossed boundaries that are
  never crossed again.
To have a child with one, and then another, to be together
  When presidents die or friends are taken prematurely,
To share a thousand laughs and tears, ten thousand meals,
To say hello and goodbye, good night and good morning beyond all
  counting or remembrance,
To see each other through tragedy and desperation, to wonder what life
  means and feel a trusting form next to you,

Or hear a child's voice echoing over a summer afternoon,
To know that weeks soon pass like months, and months years,
To know that yesterday will not return and tomorrow is not forever.
It is not love I now fear, but a life without it, and every breath I breathe
   from this moment will hold it in mind and heart,
In the very depths of my loneliness and every least dream I still have to
   share.
More than anything else, I want to hold you in my arms, gently,
   Beyond sex and security, prestige and triumph,
To say once and for all, "I love you," and mean it from the top of my
   head to the depths of my soul.
This is the love that casts out fear, that makes life worth living,
That takes a man and woman on the earth and lifts them finally above
   every power or pain that could wound them.
I have seen so many sights, heard so many words, but none as beautiful
As the sight and sound of a man and woman of mature years,
   Who say with their every act, their eyes and all their being:
      "I love you!"

Of Values

I learned about life
  From a child I hurt,
  From a woman I loved and made sad.
I learned about life
  From a feeble man's steps,
  From a friend I once thought I had.
I learned about life
  From a little boy's smile,
  From a woman's devotion to me.
I learned about life
  From a brave man I knew,
  From a friend who let me be free.
I learned about life
  From the first light of dawn,
  From the tales of a sycamore tree.
I learned about life
  From an owl at night
  From the earth sharing secrets with me.
I just couldn't learn
  From other men's Christs
  Or a memory of Moses in stone.
I learned about life
  By paying its price,
  By trying to stand up alone!

To Love Someone

To love someone
   Is a purity
Far beyond being loved.
   To be loved
     Is a security
Not a strength,
    A state of some rest,
Not a passion,
    A stilling of some inquietude
That only pines the more to love.

Where Has Time Gone?

Where has time gone,
   The secret appetite that sucks away my life?
Wasn't it yesterday that I met you
   And now you are torn from me by pain and madness?
Wasn't it but a week ago I went to school
   And learned by rote all there was to know?
Now I stand belly-deep in confusion,
   My head reels in a hundred directions
   My hopes defiled
   My dreams turned to nightmares.
Is there no release from this bondage,
   No freedom from this pain?
Is there no one who can save me
   Save the poverty of myself?
I cannot lift my head or find love in my eyes,
   Only a hollow stranger who stares back at me.
Where has time gone?
Once it was so plentiful,
   Now it is but a feeble promise
      Barely made
      Barely heard
And I am terribly afraid.

There Is Nothing to Tell You

There is nothing to tell you save how much I love you.
Your voice echoes softness and some ultimate surrender,
Your nose, royal and strong, could lure my kisses forever.
It is too soon for suddenness, or sex!
I long to caress your toes, to weave love bands in your dark hair,
  To touch your shoulder and know it has time for my tears.
Most of all I want to kiss your fingers, to suck them like fine wine,
  To whisper to them words in a language I've never spoken before.
I want to caress your earlobes with the gentleness of soft rain,
  To tell you of fears I dared not tell before.
My God, I would like to be strong for you,
  Noble and protective and prepossessing.
But I am now a wounded butterfly with the wax rubbed from his wings,
  A trembling, captured swallow that can neither fly nor sing.
I want to love you because I do not know a single reason to love myself,
  Except to tell you how much I love you.

Of Liberation

Women gather
   Free to chat of impotent husbands
      and not quite forgotten lovers,
    Sharing dreams with old or new friends
      and confiding desperation,
   Baring souls and unburdening hearts,
Then leave relaxed and laughing,
   Promising to lunch again soon,
   Freed from the pain of no one knowing.

Men gather
   Free to boast of the money they've made
      or will make soon—or the women,
    Displaying how strong and controlled they are
      and unafraid of competition,
   Sharing triumphs and hiding themselves,
Then leave with a handshake and "See you around,"
   Bleeding silently within themselves,
   Bearing the pain of no one knowing.

All These Years

All these years
   I thought I was 6′3″
   With broad shoulders and tapered hips,
   With abundant charm, a future without limit,
   Wisdom beyond my experience
   And enough ardent admirers to keep the loneliness away.

Lately I have felt
   That I'm about 5′4″
   With rounded shoulders and a pot gut
   That follows me relentlessly
      —even when I'm holding it in—
   With nothing much to say to anyone
   And enough loneliness to keep the most ardent admirers away.

Now I think I'm finally satisfied
   To be 5′9½″
   With a receding hairline,
   With sags and wrinkles and a root canal,
   With a few friends
   Who decided to love me for whatever reason
   And could care less about my appearance or accomplishments
All these years.

I Looked at You

I looked at you and every childhood dream was true,
Every longing of my life fulfilled. Cynicism disappeared
And caution deserted me like a shadow of some former self.
I wanted you, not like a drowning man seeking any safety,
But like a strong man exulting in sudden sunlight when he has become
    accustomed to the clouds.
I have known beauty before
    A doe at the river
    Twilight welcoming the night
    Cold water at the end of a mountain climb.
But I cannot remember when such beauty as yours, fragile and strong
    all at once, so possessed me to recklessness and madness.
I wanted to embrace you like the river does rocks, to kiss you more
    longingly than vines twisting toward the sun.
Stupidly I asked time to wait and feared to speak, from some pain or
    wisdom, lest the vision vanish.
Even though I knew this was a transforming love that almost tore my
    heart in two,
And that I loved you far beyond the fleeting wonder of a sudden ro-
    mance,
I feared, as once I never would have, that my rapture would only seem
    the wild love of transient passion.
And like some transfigured apostle, who wanted to stay in that place
    forever, I dared not lest I frighten you away.
Time has passed and I have cursed my cowardice so long as to wonder
    if what I felt had really happened at all.
Finally I am content to know that I can still feel what I felt, no matter
    how timidly I pursued my dream.
It is enough to have loved you, all in an instant, and to know that some-
    where you walk the earth,
And that I will somehow find you, in another instant, that endures for-
    ever.

Somehow I Always Fear

Somehow I always fear
    That if I love you
The great love I longed for
    All my life
Will suddenly appear
    And I will not be ready.
Lately I wonder
    If you are my great love
And I am yours,
    And it is only in looking back
That we will know it.

Hurrying Through Life

Hurrying through life like a child
   Forever anticipating some joy tomorrow,
   Afraid to miss something
And missing damn near everything!
   Afraid to build a dream step by step
And to wait for all that is destined.
   Ready to take the instant pleasure lest we die
And missing all the simple beauty
   Of planting in the spring
   Harvesting in the summer
And of wondering and loving and dreaming all year long.
Who will teach us to walk slowly
   To grasp each moment
And to understand
   That what now is
Will never be again.

Duke

Duke's one of those graying jocks
  Still wearing his letter sweater
  With the hint of sadness in his eyes
  Telling you life hasn't been much
Since he scored three times his last game in high school
  Against Ellerton.
He loves his old lady and all that,
  Calls an eighty-five-year-old mother once a week,
  Worries about kids and grandkids,
  Looks everyone straight in the eye,
  And still carries his lunch to the same mill
    his father did.
  He plays racquet ball every week,
    bowls in winter,
  Drinks too much on Friday after work,
  Lives for the football games
    after church on Sunday.
He dies in the spring before the baseball season
  When nothing's going on.
But most of all,
  Amid statistics and point spreads,
  Ten dollars on a heavyweight champ,
    and five on a new kid who's got the goods,
That hint of sadness tells you
  That life hasn't really measured up
  Since that Friday night in high school
Duke scored three times against Ellerton.

Elmo

Elmo prays
  Not because he's got the faith
  Or because he learned about God
    At his mother's knee
    Or at a preacher's elbow.
Elmo prays
  Because he tried everything else
    Drinking
    Screwing
    Running away
    Working
  To take away the pain of being a frightened man
    Which is totally unacceptable
    Especially to women and most men.
  And none of this worked very well
  Till Elmo started talking
    To someone
    Somewhere
    Who seemed to understand.
Now Elmo prays
  Not to Jesus or Buddha
  Not to a theological God or philosophical omnipotence
  Not to a computerized and selective savior.
    Just to someone
    Somewhere
    Who seems to understand
  And likes the hell out of Elmo.

The Pope Recently

The Pope recently
   Took the Bible a step further
And said that a man
   Should not look with lust
     at his own wife.
Edna Mae O'Brien
   Who would give anything
     to be lusted after again
Wondered if the Pope
   Had discussed this matter
     with his father.

Most of the Warriors

Most of the warriors I knew
Have settled down to gardening and the morning *Times*,
  Tired of stalking ghosts
  And the melody of secret rhythms
    above the sound of traffic
    and other monotonous voices,
  Finally content to stare and wonder.

Most of the warriors I knew
Have unsaddled stallions and built a fence in the backyard,
  Weary of studying the clouds
  And the shadows creeping across mountains
    beyond the flash of neon
    and other pretentious symbols,
  Finally content to stare and wonder.

Most of the warriors I knew
Have died before their time and are forgotten
  Save in the memory of their sons
  And the dreams they seldom share
    beyond the taint of time
    and other unimportant measures
  Finally content to stare and wonder.

Aldo

Aldo always told me with that big grin of his
That life was just a kind of game
   And it really didn't matter how you lived it
   Or how you made your money—as long as you made it—
   Because the women like a guy with a lot of it,
And Aldo always liked the women.

Aldo always told me with that big laugh of his
That life was just a kind of game
   And he really didn't give a damn if Beirut perished,
   Or if Belfast, Jerusalem, and El Salvador disappeared in the sea,
   Because abalone and lobster would still taste as sweet,
And Aldo really liked his lobster.

Aldo always told me with that big wink of his
That life was just a kind of game
   That provided you as much respect as your wallet held
   And cared about you as long as you could pick up any tab,
   Because nice guys always finished last
And Aldo had never really been nice to anyone.

Thus I was surprised
 When Aldo's brother Leo died of cancer,
 And his wife Joy left him to marry a longtime friend,
 And he couldn't unload the condominiums that were supposed to fill
  his pockets forever,
That Aldo quietly killed himself in his garage without a grin
 Although he still owned Boardwalk and Park Place
 And there was a lot of time left
In the game.

Of Inflation

One thing I do like
  About inflation
  Or economic depression
  Or whatever the hell
    Economists have decided
      is happening to us,
There aren't
  Nearly as many
  Of those smug thirty-year-olds
  In their rumpled cords and XKE's
Who sold two pieces of real estate
  And act like
They just founded General Motors.

There's No Reason

There's no reason for a person with decent capital, with cleverness,
   business judgment, and the breaks,
Not to make a million dollars in the free enterprise system.
Even though the wheel has been discovered and the airplane, along
   with plastic, nylon, penicillin, skateboards, and vibrators,
No one has developed tire chains that slip on easily, false teeth and
   contact lenses that can be worn forever,
Or a successful way to paralyze barking dogs in the middle of the night.
Some people, of course, will spend their whole life complaining that
   hamburgers and French fries haven't been the same since Korea, that
   ice cream is slush and tomatoes taste more like celery every year.
And the cynics will continue to maintain that real estate can't go up,
That taxes and inflation will lead to spineless socialism, and that any-
   one over fifty can survive
Only if he buys gold, hoards food, or has generous kids.
I have refused to be daunted by such economic pessimists.
I will continue to market vigorously an electric tennis racket,
Campaigning tirelessly to make the crow as popular as the parakeet,
   and replace Santa Claus with an aging cowboy or a suitable Indian.
Granted that razor blades have been exploited, not to mention sham-
   poos, deodorants, life insurance, and God.
There's still room for two more chicken franchises, another game show,
   a self-help psychiatric kit to comfort the victims of the soaps
And a computerized talk show to argue with anyone, at any time, about
   anything.

I Feel Sad

I feel sad about my country lately
When damn near everyone I know
   Thinks it's okay to take money away
   From the disabled and the old
As long as we increase military spending
And are certain beyond all paranoia
   That we can take Russia out
   Faster and more completely than Russia can take us out.
My buddy Danny tells me that we're getting rid of the freeloaders
   And I know damn well he doesn't mean the rich people
     Who invest in feed lots they don't see or want, or
     Get oil and mineral and agricultural allowances
       They don't need or deserve.
I confess I've occasionally wondered about
   Some of the people I see with food stamps,
And I suppose I've bitched my share about welfare.
But I do notice that the most expensive restaurants are still crowded,
   The Mercedes are as common as VW's once were,
   Fifth Avenue and Rodeo Drive seem as active as ever,
While the aged and the poor seem shabbier and more defeated
   Than I've ever seen them in my lifetime,
   Too intimidated and nervous even to whisper of revolution.
I feel sad about my country lately
   Because it lost its morals somewhere between Korea and Watergate,
   And lost its heart somewhere between this recession and the last.

Now the strangers buy our banks and the immigrants our fast foods
   And we take any dollar or ruble we can get
   To satisfy an appetite as insatiable as the fear that creates it
Content to build cheap barracks and call them homes,
Content to widen the massive gulf between rich and poor,
Content above all to defend a country
   With the expensive nuclear trinkets of a paranoia
      Bred of greed and fear and most unmanly men.
I never knew a brave nation could be so reprehensible,
   That a dollar could mean so much or a life so little,
And I am very sad.

It Seems Weird

It seems weird why a man with Desmond's income
  Would choose to live on the fringe of the slums
    In a high-crime neighborhood,
  When he could afford a lovely condominium
    Or a luxury townhouse with a community pool,
    A sauna, a Jacuzzi, and a private *Nautilus*.
Well, Desmond said the condos seemed like lonely prisons,
  That he never really knew his neighbors because
    No one spoke or answered his questions,
  That he didn't need the weight room when he started walking to
    work,
  That the slums have an individual character that seems to be missing
    everywhere else,
  That the people talk and laugh because they're already in the high-
    crime district and don't have a lot to fear,
  And besides, Desmond was far more frightened by electronically
    protected boredom and well-manicured loneliness
  Than by all the muggings and robberies in the world.
It's obvious that Desmond is cracking up.

Of Course

Of course, it's hard for men like Mike O'Shea
To understand the IRA and all that bloodshed
    (which amounts to a summer weekend in Chicago)
Hard to believe in religious wars
    when he's never known anything worth fighting for,
Hard to believe in historical antagonism
    when Paul Revere is a comic in a commercial,
The Civil War is for buffs who probably have
    railroad trains set up in their basements,
And even World Wars I and II are TV series or yesterday's movies.
Of course, it's hard to believe in hunger strikes
    When you've never been a proud man
        with hungry kids and no job
    And a wife who makes do with potatoes and worn dresses.
It's hard to believe in revolution
    When your greatest pride is not paying tax
    When your only physical exhaustion is on the tennis court,
    When Selma is a vague memory and your commitment to the poor
        is to wonder if they have insurance.
Meanwhile, a prince marries in splendor and brave men die of hunger
    To announce to a deaf world that they will not live
        without the civil rights they've been promised,
    Or they cannot honorably stroke the hair of their children.
So, of course it's hard for men like Mike O'Shea
    To understand the IRA and all that bloodshed.

I Accept the Fact

I accept the fact
  That I am a child of immigrants,
  The more fortunate variety
    Who knew the language when they arrived,
So I try to find in my heart some genuine understanding
  For Vietnamese and Cubans
  Puerto Ricans and Koreans
  Chinese, Filipinos, and even the East Indians
    Who must own every other motel south of San Francisco.
But I'll be damned
  If I'll go to an open house sponsored by an Iranian
  Who paid a million cash for an old California mansion
And now wants his American neighbors
  To assist him in changing a zoning ordinance.

Here I Am

Here I am opening my mail and discovering that I am a source of hope
To a tender lady in Concord and a venerable man in Tennessee,
While I wonder in the midst of a sudden, midlife sadness,
   Who will give strength and solace to me?
All my friends seem too happy to understand, even the losers are some-
   how finding their way.
I, who apparently have everything to live for, am hard pressed to find a
   reason today.
If I were a woman it would be purely hormonal, and an understanding
   doctor would provide me with pills.
But men don't go crazy over nothing. We just shrug and make light of
   our ills.
After all, I'm the guy who played tackle football, and beat the hell out
   of Fast Eddy McGee.
I can't sit here answering my letters, begging strangers to have pity on
   me.

Damn!

Damn! I can't believe Jenny got married, crazy old Jenny,

And Diane's got a kid coming in November, the fourth one by three different men.

Even Betty Lou's living with a guy and packing his lunch every day like a real wife.

When I called Marlene in Oklahoma, an older man answered and sure as hell didn't act like her dad.

I tried Melody and discovered she's joined a religious order. I wasn't even sure there were any.

And Trish is in law school with barely time for lunch.

Alicia is practicing the new celibacy or worn out from when she didn't,

And Barbara has developed a three-level intimacy with her Tai-Chi instructor. A year ago she thought Tai Chi was a Mexican drink.

Virginia moved back east to Connecticut because the West is corrupt and inane—and besides all culture moves from east to west, then back. Or so she said.

Elsie is living with Denise just to see how it feels and so far it feels real good.

Bernice has joined a commune in Ohio (in Ohio?) and Drusilla is shipping dried fish from Portugal.

I do have a way of putting things off.

    I wonder if Lisa's still around . . .

I Can Remember

I can remember
   When I resisted the very first "Please don't litter" signs even as a
     small boy,
   When I refused to use zip codes for more than a year,
   And paid my traffic tickets only under threat of jail.
Even though all of that has changed, I still
   Dial information whenever I need a phone number,
   Refuse to call waiters by their first name (Hi, I'm Dale),
   Think England should get the hell out of Ireland,
   Wonder if I have to be handicapped to park anymore,
   And wish America would stop policing the world.
So there's no reason for you
   To take my resistance to marriage personally.
Obviously I have some problem with authority.

Depreciation

The only depreciation
    I've never taken
Is on our love.
    Do you think
The IRS would understand?

I Want to Lie With You

I want to lie with you covered with canvas
   in the wind,
And feel the rain beat against us.
I want to walk with you across the moor
    And feel the earth crunch under our feet,
    Knowing there is no safety or security
      anywhere in the world
Save in our love.
I do not want to see the sun for days,
   You will be my only light and I yours.
We will tear at each other in hunger and thirst,
Give in to our desperation, and admit finally
   That we will break every law on heaven and earth
Save the law of our love.
If you pause to think, it is too late,
If you stop to ask permission or the least advice,
    Then we must join the banality of the long line
    Walking where they are told,
Safely, securely, and sadly.

Of Male Liberation:
Drinking With an Old Buddy

So how long's it been? A year?
   Whatta you been up to?
      (Did you see the lungs on that one?)
You had a breakdown?
   Just couldn't put it all together? I feel for you.
      (God! Look at the ass on the one in red!)
Out of work for six months? Unbelievable pressure!
   No one to talk to?
      (Oh man, I'm in love! Get a load of that body!)
Why didn't you let me know?
   What's a buddy for?
      (Christ, I'd kill for a night with the brunette)
I still don't understand why you didn't call me?
   What's a buddy for?

Too Old

When I was seven
  I told my mother
I was too old for short pants,
And when I was in fifth grade,
  I quit wearing knickers.
Too old again.
When I was twenty-three,
  It seemed too late to start over
  In a new kind of work
Because I hated to waste two extra years of college.
So, instead, I spent ten extra years
  Working at what I didn't want to do,
Changing my way at thirty-five
  When I was too old at twenty-three.
Yesterday I decided
  That I was too old not to be
  Settled and successful
And thought maybe I'd get in some kind of work
  That might make me happier
  And have a promising future.
I called my best friend
  And asked his advice.
"Aren't you getting a little old for that?"

The Phone Company

Well, the phone company and I got into it again, despite my awareness that a little honey, etc.,

And why the hell should I create more tension in a world where Iraq is weeping like Rachel over lost warheads,

And even America is ready to kill over the baseball strike?

So I waited patiently for my "somewhere between eight and twelve" appointment,

Which only the utilities and popular prostitutes can get away with,

And even called humbly at one o'clock to announce the nonarrival of the technician,

Only to be informed soprano sweetly—after seven minutes on hold—that I will have a phone "sometime before five."

The fact I'm missing lunch and a tennis game forces me to be the slightest bit acrimonious,

And with a wounded soprano whimper I am turned over to Ma Bell's eldest baritone trouble-shooter,

The very sound of whose voice should make me willing to wait two more days.

He explains the delay as if to a kindergartener; I assert with quieter sensitivity that eight hours should accommodate even the most wayward mechanic.

With consummate fury I am locked on hold for seven more minutes.

The baritone returns, now sounding less like the six o'clock news and more like the 5th race at Pimlico,

Insisting he will hire a technician since I am obviously more important than anyone else.

I compliment his judgment briefly, spend six minutes on hold, and am finally told the technician will be at my office in thirty minutes.

After five minutes of uncomplicated wire matching and $43, I have a
    phone.

Relieved, I make my first call, then a second, only to hear an assortment
    of background noises like lunchbreak at the zoo.

I call telephone repair and am informed without hint of a smile that a
    technician will be out "somewhere between eight and twelve" the
    day after tomorrow.

Seminars in the City

A hundred-dollar seminar
  Entitles you to free introductions
  As long as you like
    To individuals who want proper mates
    Or discreet escorts to swinging parties.
A three-hundred-dollar seminar
  Will get you over smoking
  As soon as you like
    And restore slightly scorched lungs
    To a pristine state of pulsating glory.
A five-hundred-dollar seminar
  Will teach you how to hoard real estate,
  As much as you like
    Without a genuine down payment, a net worth,
    Or even a steady job.

A thousand-dollar seminar
   Will give you a business of your own
   As big as you like
     If you develop an attitude
     Like the fast-talking lady who teaches it.

There are no ads
   That promise to make a sexually active, nonsmoking,
      property-laden, successful businessman content.
Perhaps he should give seminars.

Service Stations

I'm old enough to remember when gas stations became "service" stations,

And gentle men in pressed and colorful uniforms made you feel like you were rich and important, or at least decent,

And if the restrooms weren't spotless my dad said the hell with them even if they had the best gas in the world and took all the bugs off your windshield, which they did.

Nowadays a potbellied nurd or a surly kid stands watching me struggle with a recalcitrant gas cap, instructs me officiously to stick the hose in farther so the pneumatic seal will work, tells me how to squeegee my own windows, wonders if I need a tuneup, and then charms me with his views on America.

Somehow this malformed jerk seems responsible for OPEC, Texas, the oil depletion allowance, and most of inflation,

But despite my fury, I hold my tongue until the free flow of unsolicited opinion about America.

At that point I advise him I don't give a damn about his views on America.

I only hope he lives long enough till a gas station becomes a service station again.

Then I get in my car and absolutely refuse to pay him unless he gets off his ass and comes to the window of my car.

When he makes no move, neither do I. And when he walks off to regale another customer with his views,

I drive away and make a small contribution to the future of inflation.

I've Often Wondered

I've often wondered if there's any connection
    Between tailor-made clothes
    And ready-to-wear thoughts.
I've also wondered about
    Papal infallibility and the virgin birth,
    How anyone can watch the Indianapolis classic,
    Whether a king could be any worse than most presidents,
    If jogging women end up with breasts,
    And if the average yearly rainfall is related to sexual appetites.
Lately I've wondered about strange things
    Like guys who claim to make a great martini.
How the hell do you make a bad one?
    Leave out the gin?

Self-Taught

Well, I got my self-taught plumbing guide today from Time-Life books
  Where this guy in three colors has a big wrench and cool look just
    after he remodeled his entire bathroom
  Without spilling, swearing, or cracking a tile.
Since I've always been a consummate klutz like my father
  And hated those men that look at a stuttering engine and announce
    calmly that the "flugen wheel" is broken,
I studied the book carefully—damn, those are great pictures—
  Practiced my quiet, knowledgeable stare and a brow-wrinkling that
    hovered neatly between wisdom and wonder.
Mentally I repaired the plastic drainpipe—PVC to us experts—
And imagined slicing a copper pipe and soldering it to a U-joint,
  As in color illustration #34 on page 21.
Later I bought $467.89 worth of recommended tools and strutted to my
  car like *High Noon* with a holster full of wrenches, not to mention
  clamps, snips, soldering wire, pipe-cutters, and a new, easy-to-in-
  stall garbage disposal.
After studying the diagram for five minutes and checking every Time-
  Life reference under "garbage,"
I remained calm like the illustration, stared knowledgeably,
  Then went next door and prevailed upon my "flugen wheel"
    neighbor to give me an assist.

He complimented me on my tools, nodded kindly when I talked about
  gravity flow and the effect of celery stalks on drains,
Then gently bade me move myself and my holster out of the way while
  he installed the disposal.
Even my father would have been proud,
  I can hardly wait until next week
    When the self-taught electrical guide arrives.

I Don't Know Why

I don't know why it bothers me
    But in the midst of the most poignant news,
    Of the shooting of a President or Pope,
    Or an earthquake in South America,
There is a commercial somewhere selling soap or cereal,
    Promising luxury or peace of mind,
    Or an end to all offensive odors
    Except commercials.
And from time to time,
    When I wonder about my own demise,
I know that at the very moment of my passing,
Even as the word is circulated among my friends,
I will be eulogized somewhere
    By an improved tomato sauce
    Or whiter teeth.

Ernie

There's gotta be a law against a guy like Ernie,
I mean, one drink
   And he's the happiest sonofabitch in the world.
It just ain't right
   To drive a delivery truck most of your life,
   To be married three times
      And have kids by four different women,
   Not to know your father
      And to call your mother once or twice a year,
   To greet whores and nuns, kids and councilmen
      With the same broad grin,
   To ignore church and never to have opened a Bible,
      Or even wondered about it,
   Not to fear death
      And have no opinions about an afterlife,
   To think the sun, moon, stars, and a summer day
      Are your private endowment,
And to be the happiest sonofabitch in the world
   After just one drink.

Somewhere Along the Way

Somewhere along the way
A persistent voice taught me I was in competition
  With every other man in the world.
I listened carefully
  And learned the lesson well.
It was not enough
  To find a loving wife and have average, happy kids,
  To see a sunrise and wonder at an eclipsing moon,
  To enjoy a meal and catch a trout in a silent, silver river,
  To picnic in a meadow at the top of a mountain
    Or ride horses along the rim of a hidden lake,
  To laugh like a child at midnight
    And to still wonder about the falling stars.
It was only enough
  To be admired and powerful and to rush from one success to an-
    other,
  To barely see faces or hear voices, to ignore beauty and forget about
    music,
  To reduce everything and everybody to a stereo color pattern on the
    way to some new triumph,
  To rest in no victory, but to create new and more demanding goals
    even as I seem to succeed,
  Until finally I was estranged and exhausted, victorious and joyless,
    successful and ready to abandon life.

Then somewhere along the way
  I remembered the laugh of a child I once knew,
  I saw a familiar boy wandering joyously in the woods,
  I felt a heart pounding with excitement at the birth of a new day,
  Until I was in competition with no one and life was clear again,
Somewhere along the way.

A World Too Vast and Confusing

A world too vast and confusing ever to understand
　　Save in the damp hair of a sleeping child
　　Or a cat rubbing against my leg.
Where are the theories that once sustained me?
The dreams of some longed-for success
　　Or assorted Christs hanging from trees
　　And rising from the cold, damp earth?
I have seen death too many times and fail to comprehend its mercy.
Even the fiercest rain finally stops pounding,
The frozen, brittle ground finally thaws under spring's persistence,
The daffodils always startle me as if I had again lost faith in their
　　resurrection.
But what of mine?
Who can heal the deepest, rawest fear that does not surrender to
　　religious wooing?
Even as I write in the middle of some lost night,
　　The dogs have cornered a trembling deer,
　　Five of them crowding and circling like cowards,
　　　　Growling their collective courage at some sudden display of
　　　　　timidity.
I hate the dogs that snarl and surround,
Traveling through life in packs like coyotes,
　　Strong in numbers, nothing by themselves.

But what of one who has no pack
    Save a friend or lover, a sweating child, a cat rubbing against his leg
        in some silent accord
    With warmth and history and passing time,
And a vague awareness that what little I possess
    Is mine?

On the Death of a Beloved Brother

Dearest brother, there are no words to encompass my love!
I never knew you well enough till now and want so desperately
   To tell you that all the years were as nothing.
You are still the big brother you were, only now I know
   Your child's fear and can tell you of mine.
Now I know there is only childhood, never really changing,
   Never really growing or going anywhere but in circles.
I can still smell your football sweat on the crisp Saturday mornings
   Mingling painfully with the odor of your death.
I can still see your shy, gaped-tooth child's smile
   Mingling with that final, startled grimace of your passing.
And I know that you were still the child you'd always been.
Why did you have to die?
   Even today I saw drooling old women and opaque old men
      Shuffling along on their walkers without a reason to live,
      Paying no attention to a catbird's song or a falling leaf.

My God, you loved so much!
  Your dog and forever pregnant cat, spring rains and the Mexicans
    who tended your trees and flowers,
  Your roses and the *LA Times,* gin rummy and still brilliant con-
    versation at midnight,
  Your roasts and TV, your bourbon and sprawling land,
  Football and the NBA, oysters and kippers, and me.
Why should you die when the arrogant internist who misdiagnosed still
  lives?
  Or the greedy radiologist who glanced through his magazine while
    your proud red hair fell out?
  Or the lying oncologist who promised something to justify his fee?
Why should you die and leave me without your face? Your voice?
  Your touch? And most of all, that proud smile like our father's?
I wish I had held you longer and looked forever into your eyes,
  Told you that we were still children together on Oakland Drive,
    Cuddling in the big maple bed against the Midwestern cold,
    Fishing Michigan's streams and wandering Canada's lakes,
    Laughing away our priesthood that night in New Orleans
      And dancing it away on New Year's Eve in Miami.
But more than all of this I only wish you were coming back—even for a
  weekend—
So I could tell you how much I always loved you.

When I Met You

When I met you
  The smog was standing like buttermilk,
  Transforming shrouded mountains
    Into impatient eavesdroppers.
  Disappointed stars were waiting to be admitted
    Like curious children at a bedroom door,
  The moon was corn-colored and passionate
    Like an exotic bride attending her beloved.
  Even the crow who announced that anyone was alive
  Or wanted to be
    Rehearsed his nuptial baritone.
We heard the weather reports, hysterics gasping about
    Ten-stage alerts and foul air.
But I would not trade that night
  For all the clean air and endless stars
  That waited respectfully
    Offstage
When I met you.

I Cannot Begin Again

I cannot begin again
   To study the veins of granite rocks
   And explore the anxiety of clouds.
   To relearn the secrets of trees
   And see the shadows of mountains.
There are too many forms already seen,
   Too many sounds heard too often,
   Too many dreams etched in my memory
      like water scarring ancient foundations.
I have already built a home in my heart
   Where sadness is only as frequent as the rain
   And joy as unpredictable as sunlight.
Come live there with me before I die of loneliness!
Beyond the curves and crest of some unwrinkled innocence,
   I only want the wrinkles that I wrinkled,
   I want to kiss the scars that my own dagger left,
   I want to see the crow's-feet
      And to know that I am the crow that walked across your face.
But I cannot begin again.

Maybe Love Will Never Come

Maybe love will never come
   Like I planned so fervently and long
      Gazing at waitresses
      Studying freeways
      Scratching and digging at every opportunity.
But I will have known a quiet time
   On a moonlit night like this
      Where the Big Dipper
      Sits steaming on a stove of clouds
      And I know for an instant
   That I am really alive.
Maybe love will never come
   Like I planned so fervently and long.
For some it never does, you know.
   I see them gathered on bus corners
      Maids and practical nurses
      Clerks at department stores
      Janitors with lunches they packed themselves.
   Love is not everything, you know
      There are ballgames and hungry squirrels in the park
      Laughing children and bold bluejays everywhere,
      Dawn's invitation and a sunset's promise.

But as long as I am alive
  I will not believe
    That love will never come
Because I have planned so fervently and long.

You Could Have Told Me Anything

You could have told me anything
    And I would not have heard,
But when your neck trembled as you tried to talk,
    Trembled just above the throat
    Trembled involuntarily like a child,
Then my heart broke and I damned everything
    I've ever stood for.
What kind of man is this
    Who makes your throat tremble?
Like the sparrow I killed with my BB gun
    A hundred years ago.
I doubt the gods forgive those
Who make a tiny neck tremble
    Tremble just above the throat,
    Tremble involuntarily.
More eloquent, passionate, touching,
    Than anything you've ever said to me,
And you unaware that you said it.

Love Was Not to Come Like This

Love was not to come like this,
   After effort and in ambush.
It was to happen on a rainy night,
   Me looking suavely
      Over the collar of my London Fog
   And streetlights glowing rainbows
      On the silver pavement.
It was to be East Side New York,
   Or North Beach San Francisco.
   At least Sandburg Village in Chicago.
I was to kiss you coolly, eyes open in the mist,
   To feel you falter and dissolve in my arms,
   Like all those chestnut, full-breasted fantasies of mine.
There were not to be
   Those quarrels and silent nights,
   Distances and madness and untouched food,
   Endless conversations and separations,
   Certainly no untimely deaths or betrayal by friends.
Love would never be a final surrender,
   Always a sudden beginning,
Love would be an adolescent surprise,
   Not a midlife recompense
   Or a graying afterthought.
But assuredly, love was not to come like this,
   After effort
   And in ambush.

Maybe If I Loved You More

Maybe if I loved you more
   I could take away sadness lost in childhood crevices,
   I could bring the familiar glow of love to your whole being,
     Caress away the fear on your face, dissolve unshed tears,
   With dreams I once thought too childish to share.

Maybe if I loved you more
   I could kiss away the anxious chatter of your loneliness
   I could rouse in you new courage with my laughter
     Transform weariness to passion, re-create in you
   The wonder I saw when first I loved you.

Maybe if I loved you more
   I would not have to walk away again in loneliness
   Or wander off in painful hope that someone will finally love me.
     I could simply go home and take you silently in my arms
   As once I did so easily.

Maybe if I loved you more
   I could admit hurts and failures and morning terrors,
   I could begin to merge my secret despair into new hope,
     Loving without devouring, whispering without intruding,
   Knowing that we will be together until the end.

Maybe if I loved you more
 I would not have to know the empty silence and prolonged death,
 The pain of separation, the hurt of knowing how much I hurt you.
  Maybe all the talk and explanations
  Maybe all the questions and words and confrontations are really
   unnecessary.
  Maybe it's not so complex at all.
Maybe if I loved you more . . .

When All the Lights

When all the lights of yesterday have disappeared
And all the echoes of childhood have been forgotten,
When the sky is shrouded to deny even the morning sun its splendor,
And the ocean is as dull as an inland lake,
When even my love cannot rescue me from the indescribable pain of
    emptiness and the pointlessness of life,
When a good meal or a football game cannot stir me,
And nothing I've done or will do can appease the wrath of an unknown
    demon who tortures me
For something someone else must have done,
And mocks my every struggle to make life warm and joyful again,
When finally there is no hope,
I admit to you my terror,
   Surrender to my own helplessness,
And a feeble light creeps around the edges of the clouds.

Raised As I Was

Raised as I was with devils and angels and a giant computer in the sky,
I used to worry about God and afterlife and unquenchable fire.
Unlike Pascal, I finally decided that if God is as mean and petty
As mean and petty Christians say he is, then it's just a crapshoot even
   for mean and petty Christians.
And if God is a meticulous and malevolent moron
Who conditions salvation on Sunday morning TV terms,
Then a lot of Jews, Buddhists, Muhammadans, and guys like me are in
   deep trouble.
Which is probably why a lot of decent people refuse to believe in God.
Since I can't accept that option with any great composure,
I decided to create my own theology like everyone else.
Granted I don't yet have a bible or a sacred mountain,
Not to mention my own TV show or even embossed stationery and a
   box number which is how anything worthwhile begins,
I do have a very friendly God who loves and understands everyone,
And has provided an afterlife which matches Muhammad's wildest
   dreams.
Now my friend Dubie says that I'm crazy not to face the fact that there
   may not be such a God or such an afterlife,
And I asked Dubie when facing facts had anything to do with anything.
As I look over the world, people who seem the happiest are the ones
   who are sure there is an afterlife,
Or those who are convinced there isn't one.
It's the wonderers who do all the worrying.
Dubie's going to get me a P.O. box tomorrow.

The Old Bachelor

The old bachelor used to be cute
  A decade or two ago.
  Now he makes me sad,
Ordering his banana split with marshmallow and announcing
  He's on a diet.
He puts his spoon in his ear and someone chuckles, not
  Like they used to
When he was somebody with something to say.
He tries the same old tricks on waitresses, pinching and things
    That used to work when his teeth were as white as his hair
    And his shoulders as broad as his memory of all the things
      Nobody cares about.
No one really knows whether to grin at him or shoot him.
The trouble is,
  It doesn't make much difference to anyone.
  Even the old bachelor.
Maybe I'll get married tomorrow.

The Therapist

"Was that the year you hurt your ankle?"
   "Hm? Then it must be the Wednesday morning lady at ten.
"But you're a taurus?
   "No? Well I guess it's Thursday at two-thirty.
"Anyway, I like your meatloaf.
   "Do you use rosemary?
"Damn! You are Rosemary!
   "How thoughtless of me."

Eddie and Edna

Eddie and Edna Ficcolo made up their minds that they were not gonna
  kill themselves forever, raising kids and making a living like everybody else in Racine, Wisconsin,
So Eddie built houses in ninety days while Edna nursed babies, sold
  drapes, and did Eddie's books far into the night
Until the kids were finally raised and they had enough money to live in
  a houseboat in San Diego
Where they continued to build tract houses and sew drapes until they
  had so damn much money there was no reason to work anymore.
So in a few months they began talking in the morning about what
  they'd had for dinner,
Wondered why the mail was fifteen minutes late and other exciting
  things like wasn't there more traffic lately in the bay
And didn't the seagulls seem darker than the year before? And maybe
They'd go skiing in Park City after Christmas, but somehow they
  couldn't get up the energy
Because gradually it could take a whole morning to have breakfast, read
  the *LA Times*, clean the houseboat, and find two brass screws that fell
  out of a piece of molding in the kitchen.
Television, formerly a best friend, became a dull enemy and even the
  LA Times seemed as predictable and depressing as the evening news.
So they played more cards and hid their disappointment from friends
  in Racine or even San Diego who dreamed of the day when they
  could have their own houseboat and know a tern from a gull and
  name three species of sandpipers.

What was not included in the dream was boredom, insomnia, impotence, insecurity, rapid aging, constipation, dull eyes, not to mention a lot of bird shit on top of the houseboat.

Finally after ten years, a few weeks short of Eddie's sixtieth birthday, they moved north, bought some land and began building houses again.

Edna sewed drapes and worked in a travel agency which gave her a reason to get up in the morning.

After two years, there was no boredom, constipation, or insomnia.

Sunday was reserved for sex and racquet ball, and two pairs of dull eyes began to look as alive as a coyote's.

After five years, when the houses were not selling and the travel agency was as boring as three days and two nights in Tijuana,

They wondered if they shouldn't give it all up and buy a houseboat in San Francisco Bay.

I Have Not Felt Such Longing

I have not felt such longing before.
Your very absence makes me angry
   That anything in the world can keep us apart.
I am weary of respecting job or time or responsibilities.
My God! I have seen jobs dissolved, time disappear
   And responsibilities carried to the grave.
There is always someone else to work or care for,
   But no one else to love.
Do you not understand? There is only love!
Must I be madly in love only in my fantasies?
Does every reality return home for her children,
   To collect the mail or answer a wrong number?
It's always a wrong number when you are in love.
Love cannot look back for such will never come again.
All else has another chance:
   A child, a job, a parent, a friend.
Only love must respect the moment.
And when it is ignored or qualified or compromised,
   Then it is never the same again.
It is only passing the time,
   However comfortably and well.

Duane

Duane's an entrepreneur with four dollars in his wallet and enough
  property to house a Cambodian village.
His net worth, he tells me, even though I didn't ask, is three million,
  and likely to be four
    If he can refinance an apartment house
    Trade twenty acres for a run-down motel
    And convert the motel into cheap apartments
For those who live from hand to mouth and still have time to enjoy a
  sunset.
When I listen to Duane and watch him spread out his paper wealth like
  the last peanut butter in the jar,
When I hear him brag of paying no taxes and hoarding silver,
I'm damn glad I have a fireplace, a bottle of wine, coffee in the morning
  and a crisp October day,
Glad that my happiness is not a condominium conversion away.
I'm also glad that I have twenty bucks to lend Duane until his cash flow
  improves.

Time

Once I thought
    Time was my master, demanding that I rise up before I was ready,
    Urging me to herd cattle when I was still wondering about planting
        wheat,
    Establishing impatient deadlines when there was no reason to hurry
        at all,
    Forcing me in new directions when I was still enjoying the old.
Now I know
    Time is a liar who promises to reward impatience and hard work,
    Time is a tyrant with a horror of old age and an obsession with death.
Now I know
    Time means nothing
    Because neither a day nor a lifetime
        Is long enough to love you.

Storybook Love

You want a storybook love manufactured a century or two ago in
   England, or yesterday in Hollywood,
Where palm trees never weep, but sigh only of silken sheets, and even
   desert sands whisper of nothing but soft seduction.
You do not want our love
   Conceived in adolescent hunger,
   Born and bred in pain and confusion.
"Life should be simpler," you say.
   Who made it simple?
Don't you know
   That life slows and wrinkles and finally disappears?
Don't you know
   That the young writhe to supplant the old
     and yesterday's hero is mumbling on a screened-in porch?
Don't you know that I was taught
   To confront and conquer every man I met?
   To seduce and bed down every woman I could get?
Don't you know that I have made my tired way here
   Only after looking down a hundred other man-made roads?
Storybook love tells romantic girls of any age
   What they want to hear.
I can only offer a fragile man's love,
   Wounded by time and fear.

Indifferent Days

Indifferent days
  Cordially passing the time,
Silent nights surveying private spaces,
Lives brushing by
  In peaceful, distant rhyme,
Separate dreams concealed on shrouded faces.

No longer looking
  At each other's unpublished eyes,
Not even noticing what we're wearing.
Morning and evening
  Without contention or surprise,
Barely intruding on some inner staring.

At what instant
  Did an unbroken closeness end
With silent nights surveying private spaces?
At what moment
  Did each of us lose our finest friend
With separate dreams concealed on shrouded faces?

The Price of Coffee

The price of coffee's gone up
With an end to loneliness
  And the promise of love in the morning.
All it costs is your life
  And endless hours of boredom
Unless you're willing to wage a war
For personal freedom
  And the release of all those thoughts
You've hidden so well.

There Are No Rules Anymore

There are no rules anymore,
    The stars are unpredictable,
        The tides have betrayed the puzzled moon.
    I have learned to loathe the imperturbable sun
        That refused to heal you.
Were there a gentle, loving God
    With any function save madness on the earth
        He would know that your departure
            Is beyond all replacement.
        He would have taken a life grown stale,
            A weary, embittered heart,
Not the brave and brilliant spirit of an unlived life.
I have died before, but never like this.
    Finally I am left alone
        To find solace for my own pain
            Without a hint of wisdom or the least recourse,
For there are no rules anymore.

90

I Am Terrorized

I am terrorized by your tears
As if some god has commissioned me
   To dry the eyes of the world
   And leave it loved and grinning in my wake.
There is so much pain
   Of unwanted children and middle-aged men with fear in their eyes,
   Of unloved women who sob and scream for a daddy in the night,
   Of old folks sitting sadly on the porch, watching life wander relent-
     lessly away,
   Of failed artists and unwanted actors with lowered eyes and trem-
     bling lips.
I am only strong enough to understand my own tears,
   To soothe my own silent screams,
But I am terrorized by your tears,
As if some god has commissioned me to dry the eyes of the world.

Love Endures

Love endures beyond time or place
   And mocks the frightened rumors
   Of what should or shouldn't be.
Love listens only to one's own heart
   No matter what friends or family
   Or the computerized voices say.
Love dares to dream
   Beyond all calculations
   That only sanctify what always was.
Love is an uncharted madness
   Reserved for the few
   Who are forever restless
Until every light has been turned on
   Every note sounded across mountains
   Every echoing whisper has been answered
   And every loving promise
Is eternally fulfilled.

Most of All

Most of all
  I like the trees,
    Rooted in the earth,
    Silent and unafraid to be alone,
  Proud in a forest
  Or strong and solitary in a meadow,
Refusing to fall until the very end.
If I were to be born again,
  It would not be with Jesus
    Or his sacred rivals,
  Not with a grinning therapist
    Who has been shaped
      By what I have discarded.
I want to be born again with the trees
  Under sun and sky.
To wake up every morning
  And never wonder why.

Some Vision

Some vision takes possession tonight
And life is no more real than dreams.
Some mist rises to soften each memory
And truth is whatever it seems.
Faces I loved are faded beyond recall,
Intensity's a language I no longer understand.
I'm older now, who knows if wiser?
But slower to believe what's obviously at hand.
Sunrise is more important than the morning news,
Baseball scores as meaningful as inflation's rise,
My own persistent yearnings more valid now,
Time more relentless than all the strident cries.
Redeemers come, redeemers go, preachers everywhere,
Clever lies and rock-hard eyes and death is in the air.
Jesus saves and interest pays and love is still as rare.

About the Author

JAMES KAVANAUGH lives in Los Gatos, California, where he is the director of the *James Kavanaugh Institute*, a forum for "Searchers" who are looking for "all that life has to offer." A licensed clinical psychologist, philosopher, lecturer and poet, he and his professional staff offer seminars and workshops for men and women throughout America and Canada "who are ambitious for life itself, for everything beautiful it can provide." Much of his free time is spent in the Sierra foothills outside Nevada City, California—in the gold mining country. He lectures and reads poetry at colleges, enjoys trout fishing, tennis, wandering, oceans, forests and the mountains. For information about the *James Kavanaugh Institute*, write to Box 189, Nevada City, California 95959.

An LP Recording of James Kavanaugh reading from his classic *There Are Men too Gentle to Live Among Wolves* (with an original score by Elmer Bernstein) is available for $7.95 from James Kavanaugh, 15001 National Avenue, Los Gatos, Cal. 95030.

95